Hymns for the Use of the University of Oxford in St. Mary's Church

Anatiposi

Anonymous

Hymns for the Use of the University of Oxford in St. Mary's Church

Reprint of the original, first published in 1872.

1st Edition 2023 | ISBN: 978-3-38213-032-9

Anatiposi Verlag is an imprint of Outlook Verlagsgesellschaft mbH.

Verlag (Publisher): Outlook Verlag GmbH, Zeilweg 44, 60439 Frankfurt, Deutschland
Vertretungsberechtigt (Authorized to represent): E. Roepke, Zeilweg 44, 60439 Frankfurt, Deutschland
Druck (Print): Books on Demand GmbH, In de Tarpen 42, 22848 Norderstedt, Deutschland

HYMNS

FOR THE USE OF THE

UNIVERSITY OF OXFORD

IN ST. MARY'S CHURCH

Oxford

AT THE CLARENDON PRESS

1872

ADVENT.

I.

THAT day of wrath, that dreadful day
When heaven and earth shall pass away,
What power shall be the sinner's stay?
How shall he meet that dreadful day?

When, shrivelling like a parchèd scroll,
The flaming heavens together roll;
When louder yet, and yet more dread,
Swells the high trump that wakes the dead;

O! on that day, that wrathful day,
When man to judgment wakes from clay,
Be Thou the trembling sinner's stay,
Though heaven and earth shall pass away!

II.

DIES iræ, dies illa
Solvet sæclum in favilla,
Crucis explicans vexilla.

Quantus tremor est futurus,
Quando Judex est venturus,
Cuncta stricte discussurus.

Tuba, mirum spargens sonum
Per sepulchra regionum,
Coget omnes ante thronum.

Liber scriptus proferetur,
In quo totum continetur,
De quo mundus judicetur.

Judex ergo quum sedebit,
Quidquid latet, apparebit,
Nil inultum remanebit.

Quid sum miser tum dicturus,
Quem patronum rogaturus,
Quum vix justus sit securus?

Rex tremendæ majestatis,
Qui salvandos salvas gratis,
Salva me, Fons pietatis.

Recordare, Jesu pie,
Quod sum causa Tuæ viæ;
Ne me perdas illa die!

Quærens me sedisti lassus,
Redemisti crucem passus:
Tantus labor non sit cassus.

Oro supplex et acclinis,
Cor contritum quasi cinis:
Gere curam mei finis.

III.

LO! He comes, with clouds descending,
  Once for favoured sinners slain:
Thousand thousand saints attending
  Swell the triumph of His train:
      Alleluia!
  God appears, on earth to reign!

Every eye shall now behold Him,
  Robed in dreadful majesty;
Those who set at nought and sold Him,
  Pierced, and nailed Him to the Tree,
      Deeply wailing,
  Shall the true Messiah see.

Every island, sea, and mountain,
  Heaven and earth shall flee away;
All who hate Him must, confounded,
  Hear the trump proclaim the day;
      Come to judgment!
  Come to judgment, come away!

Now redemption, long expected,
  See in solemn pomp appear;
All His saints, by man rejected,
  Now shall meet Him in the air:
      Alleluia!
  See the day of God appear!

Yea, Amen! let all adore Thee,
  High on Thine eternal throne:
Saviour, take the power and glory;
  Claim the kingdom for Thine own:
      O, come quickly,
  Everlasting God, come down!

IV.

HARK, the glad sound! the Saviour comes,
  The Saviour promised long;
Let every heart prepare a throne,
  And every voice a song!

He comes, the prisoners to release
  In Satan's bondage held;
The gates of brass before Him burst,
  The iron fetters yield.

He comes, from thickest films of vice
  To clear the mental ray,
And on the eye-balls of the blind
  To pour celestial day.

He comes, the broken heart to bind,
  The bleeding soul to cure,
And with the treasures of His grace
  To enrich the humble poor.

Our glad Hosannas, Prince of Peace,
  Thy welcome shall proclaim,
And heaven's eternal arches ring
  With Thy beloved name.

V.

GREAT GOD, what do I see and hear?
  The end of things created:
The Judge of mankind doth appear,
  On clouds of glory seated:
The trumpet sounds, the graves restore
The dead which they contained before;
  Prepare, my soul, to meet Him.

The dead in Christ are first to rise
  At that last trumpet's sounding;
Caught up to meet Him in the skies,
  With joy their Lord surrounding:
No gloomy fears their souls dismay;
His presence sheds eternal day
  On those prepared to meet Him.

Far over space, to distant spheres,
  The lightnings are prevailing;
The ungodly rise, and all their tears
  And sighs are unavailing:
The day of grace is past and gone;
They shake before the Judge's throne,
  All unprepared to meet Him.

Great Judge, to Thee our prayers we pour,
  In deep abasement bending;
O shield us through that last dread hour,
  Thy wondrous love extending:
May we, in this our trial day,
With faithful hearts Thy word obey,
  And thus prepare to meet Thee.

VI.

WHEN came in flesh the Incarnate Word,
  The heedless world slept on,
And only simple shepherds heard
  That God had sent His Son.

When comes the Saviour at the last,
  From west to east shall shine
The awful pomp, and earth aghast
  Shall tremble at the sign.

Then shall the pure in heart be blest;
  As mild He comes to them,
As when upon the Virgin's breast
  He lay at Bethlehem:

As mild to meek-eyed love and faith;
  Only more strong to save;
Strengthened, by having bowed to death,
  By having burst the grave.

Lord! who could dare see Thee descend
  In state, unless he knew
Thou art the sorrowing sinner's Friend,
  The gracious, and the true?

Dwell in our hearts, O Saviour blest!
  So shall Thine Advent dawn
'Twixt us and Thee, our bosom-Guest,
  Be but the veil withdrawn.

VII.

ON Jordan's bank the Baptist's cry
Announces that the Lord is nigh;
Come then, and hearken, for he brings
Glad tidings from the King of kings.

Then cleansed be every Christian breast,
And furnished for so great a guest;
Yea, let us each our hearts prepare
For Christ to come and enter there.

For Thou art our salvation, Lord,
Our refuge, and our great reward;
Without Thy grace our souls must fade,
And wither like a flower decayed.

Stretch forth Thine hand to heal our sore,
And make us rise to fall no more;
Once more upon Thy people shine,
And fill the world with love divine.

To Him who left the throne of heaven
To save mankind, all praise be given;
Like praise be to the Father done,
And Holy Spirit, Three in One.

VIII.

A FEW more years shall roll,
A few more seasons come,
And we shall be with those that rest
Asleep within the tomb:
Then, O my Lord, prepare
My soul for that great day;
O wash me in Thy precious blood,
And take my sins away.

A few more suns shall set
O'er these dark hills of time,
And we shall be where suns are not,
A far serener clime:
Then, O my Lord, prepare
My soul for that blest day;
O wash me in Thy precious blood,
And take my sins away.

A few more storms shall beat
On this wild rocky shore,
And we shall be where tempests cease,
And surges swell no more:
Then, O my Lord, prepare
My soul for that calm day;
O wash me in Thy precious blood,
And take my sins away.

A few more struggles here,
A few more partings o'er,
A few more toils, a few more years,
And we shall weep no more:
Then, O my Lord, prepare
My soul for that bright day;
O wash me in Thy precious blood.
And take my sins away.

'Tis but a little while
And He shall come again,
Who died that we might live, who lives
That we with Him may reign:
Then, O my Lord, prepare
My soul for that glad day;
O wash me in Thy precious blood,
And take my sins away.

CHRISTMAS.

IX.

RING out, ye crystal spheres,
Once bless our human ears,
(If ye have power to touch our senses so,)
And let your silver chime
Move in melodious time;
And let the base of heaven's deep organ blow:
And with your ninefold harmony
Make up full consort to the angelic symphony.

For if such holy song
Enwrap our fancy long,
Time will run back, and fetch the age of gold;
And speckled vanity
Will sicken soon and die,
And leprous sin will melt from earthly mould;
And hell itself will pass away,
And leave her dolorous mansions to the peering day.

Yea, truth and justice then
Will down return to men,
Orbed in a rainbow; and, like glories wearing,
Mercy will sit between,
Throned in celestial sheen,
With radiant feet the tissued clouds down steering;
And heaven, as at some festival,
Will open wide the gates of her high palace hall.

X.

ADESTE fideles,
Læte triumphantes,
Venite, venite in Bethlehem;
Natum videte
Regem Angelorum;
Venite adoremus Dominum.

Deum de Deo,
Lumen de Lumine,
Gestant Puellæ viscera;
Deum verum,
Genitum, non factum,
Venite adoremus Dominum.

Cantet nunc Io
Chorus Angelorum,
Cantet nunc aula cœlestium,
Gloria in excelsis Deo,
Venite adoremus Dominum.

Ergo qui natus
Die hodierna,
Jesu, Tibi sit gloria;
Patris æterni
Verbum Caro factum;
Venite adoremus Dominum.

XI.

ECCE quem vates vetustis
  Concinebant sæculis,
Quem prophetarum fideles
  Paginæ spoponderant,
Emicat promissus olim;
  Cuncta conlaudent eum,
    Sæculorum sæculis.

Psallat altitudo cœli,
  Psallite omnes Angeli,
Quidquid est virtutis unquam
  Psallat in laudem Dei,
Nulla linguarum silescat,
  Vox et omnis consonet,
    Sæculorum sæculis.

Macte Judex mortuorum,
  Macte Rex viventium,
Dexter assidens Parenti
  Summa nactus robora,
Omnium venturus inde
  Justus ultor criminum,
    Sæculorum sæculis.

Te senes et Te juventus,
  Parvulorum Te chorus,
Turba matrum virginumque,
  Simplices puellulæ,
Voce concordes pudicis
  Perstrepant concentibus,
      Sæculorum sæculis.

Tibi, Christe, sit cum Patre
  Hagioque Spiritu,
Hymnus, melos, laus perennis,
  Gratiarum actio,
Honor, virtus, et victoria,
  Regnum æternaliter,
      Sæculorum sæculis.

XII.

HARK! the herald-angels sing
Glory to the new-born King,
Peace on earth, and mercy mild,
God and sinners reconciled:
Joyful, all ye nations, rise,
Join the triumph of the skies;
Universal nature say,
Christ the Lord is born to-day.
    Hark! the herald-angels sing
    Glory to the new-born King.

Christ, by highest heaven adored,
Christ, the everlasting Lord,
Late in time behold Him come,
Offspring of a Virgin's womb:
Veiled in flesh the Godhead see,
Hail the Incarnate Deity!
Pleased as Man with man to dwell,
Jesus our Emmanuel.
    Hark! the herald-angels sing
    Glory to the new-born King.

Hail, the heavenly Prince of Peace,
Hail, the Sun of Righteousness!
Light and life to all He brings,
Risen with healing in His wings:

Mild He lays His glory by,
Born that man no more may die,
Born to raise the sons of earth,
Born to give them second birth.
    Hark! the herald-angels sing
    Glory to the new-born King.

XIII.

WHILE shepherds watched their flocks by night
All seated on the ground,
The angel of the Lord came down,
And glory shone around.

" Fear not," said he, (for mighty dread
Had seized their troubled mind;)
" Glad tidings of great joy I bring
" To you and all mankind.

" To you, in David's town, this day
" Is born of David's line
" The Saviour, who is Christ the Lord;
" And this shall be the sign.

" The heavenly Babe you there shall find
" To human view displayed,
" All meanly wrapt in swathing bands,
" And in a manger laid."

Thus spake the seraph; and forthwith
Appeared a shining throng
Of angels, praising God, and thus
Addressed their joyful song:

" All glory be to God on high,
" And to the earth be peace;
" Good-will henceforth from heaven to men
" Begin, and never cease!"

EPIPHANY.

XIV.

SPLENDOR Paternæ gloriæ,
De luce lucem proferens,
Primordiis lucis novæ
Diem dies illuminans:

Verusque Sol, illabere,
Micans nitore perpeti:
Jubarque sancti Spiritûs
Infunde nostris sensibus.

Lætus dies hic transeat,
Pudor sit ut diluculum,
Fides velut meridies,
Crepusculum mens nesciat.

Qui Te revelas Gentibus,
Jesu, Tibi sit gloria,
Cum Patre cumque Spiritu
In sempiterna sæcula.

XV.

JESU dulcis memoria,
Dans vera cordi gaudia,
Sed super mel et omnia
Ejus dulcis præsentia.

Nil canitur suävius,
Nil auditur jucundius,
Nil cogitatur dulcius
Quam Jesus Dei Filius.

Jesu, spes pœnitentibus,
Quam pius es petentibus,
Quam bonus Te quærentibus!
Sed quid invenientibus?

Jesus, dulcedo cordium,
Fons veri, lumen mentium,
Excedens omne gaudium
Et omne desiderium.

Nec lingua valet dicere
Nec litera exprimere,
Expertus potest credere,
Quid sit Jesum diligere.

XVI.

HOW sweet the Name of Jesus sounds
In a believer's ear!
It soothes his sorrows, heals his wounds,
And drives away his fear.

It makes the wounded spirit whole,
And calms the troubled breast;
'Tis manna to the hungry soul,
And to the weary rest.

Jesus, the rock on which I build,
My shield and hiding-place,
My never-failing treasury, filled
With boundless stores of grace.

Weak is the effort of my heart,
And cold my warmest thought;
But, when I see Thee as Thou art,
I'll praise Thee as I ought.

Till then, I would Thy love proclaim
With every fleeting breath;
And may the music of Thy name
Refresh my soul in death!

XVII.

O LOVE, who formedst me to wear
The image of Thy Godhead here;
Who soughtest me with tender care
Through all my wanderings wild and drear;
O Love, I give myself to Thee,
Thine ever, only Thine to be.

O Love, who ere life's earliest dawn
On me Thy choice hast gently laid;
O Love, who here as Man wast born,
And wholly like to us wast made;
O Love, I give myself to Thee,
Thine ever, only Thine to be.

O Love, who once in time wast slain,
Pierced through and through with bitter woe;
O Love, who wrestling thus didst gain
That we eternal joy might know;
O Love, I give myself to Thee,
Thine ever, only Thine to be.

O Love, who lovest me for aye,
Who for my soul dost ever plead;
O Love, who didst my ransom pay,
Whose power sufficeth in my stead;
O Love, I give myself to Thee,
Thine ever, only Thine to be.

O Love, who once shalt bid me rise
  From out this dying life of ours;
O Love, who once o'er yonder skies
  Shalt set me in the fadeless bowers;
O Love, I give myself to Thee,
Thine ever, only Thine to be.

XVIII.

HAIL to the Lord's Anointed,
  Great David's greater Son!
Hail, in the time appointed,
  His reign on earth begun!
He comes to break oppression,
  To let the captive free,
To take away transgression,
  And rule in equity.

He comes with succour speedy,
  To those who suffer wrong;
To help the poor and needy,
  And bid the weak be strong;
To give them songs for sighing,
  Their darkness turn to light,
Whose souls, condemned and dying,
  Were precious in His sight.

Arabia's desert-ranger
  To Him shall bow the knee;
The Ethiopian stranger
  His glory come to see;
With offerings of devotion
  Ships from the isles shall meet,
To pour the wealth of ocean
  In tribute at His feet.

Kings shall fall down before Him,
  And gold and incense bring;
All nations shall adore Him,
  His praise all people sing;
For Him shall prayer unceasing,
  And daily vows ascend,
His kingdom still increasing,
  A kingdom without end.

O'er every foe victorious
  He on His throne shall rest,
From age to age more glorious,
  All blessing and all-blest;
The tide of time shall never
  His covenant remove;
His name shall stand for ever,
  That name to us is Love.

XIX.

AS with gladness men of old
Did the guiding star behold;
As with joy they hailed its light,
Leading onward, beaming bright;
So, most gracious God, may we
Evermore be led to Thee.

As with joyful steps they sped
To that lowly manger-bed,
There to bend the knee before
Him whom heaven and earth adore;
So may we with willing feet
Ever seek Thy mercy-seat.

As they offered gifts most rare
At that manger rude and bare;
So may we with holy joy,
Pure and free from sin's alloy,
All our costliest treasures bring,
Christ! to Thee our heavenly King.

Holy Jesus, every day
Keep us in the narrow way;
And, when earthly things are past,
Bring our ransomed souls at last
Where they need no star to guide,
Where no clouds Thy glory hide.

In the heavenly country bright
Need they no created light;
Thou its light, its joy, its crown,
Thou its sun which goes not down;
There for ever may we sing
Alleluias to our King.

LENT.

XX.

THY mercies manifold
  Remember, Lord, I pray:
In pity Thou art plentiful,
  And so hast been alway.

Remember not the faults
  And frailty of my youth;
Call not to mind how ignorant
  I have been of Thy truth:

Nor after my deserts
  Let me Thy mercy find;
But of Thine own benignity,
  Lord, have me in Thy mind.

XXI.

O LORD, turn not Thy face from me,
  Who lie in woeful state,
Lamenting all my sinful life
  Before Thy mercy-gate;
A gate which opens wide to those
  That do lament their sin;
Shut not that gate against me, Lord,
  But let me enter in.

I need not to confess my life
  To Thee, who best canst tell
What I have been, and what I am;
  I know Thou know'st it well:
Wherefore, to beg and to entreat,
  With tears I come to Thee,
As children that have done amiss
  Fall at their father's knee.

O Lord, I need not to repeat
  The comfort I would have;
Thou know'st, O Lord, before I ask,
  The blessing I do crave:
Mercy, good Lord, mercy I ask,
  This is the total sum;
For mercy, Lord, is all my suit;
  Lord, let Thy mercy come!

XXII.

HAVE mercy, Lord, on me,
As Thou wert ever kind;
Let me, oppressed with loads of guilt,
Thy wonted mercy find.

Wash off my foul offence,
And cleanse me from my sin;
For I confess my crime, and see
How great my guilt has been.

Make me to hear with joy
Thy kind forgiving voice;
That so the bones which Thou hast broke
May with fresh strength rejoice.

Blot out my crying sins,
Nor me in anger view;
Create in me a heart that's clean,
An upright mind renew.

Withdraw not thou Thy help,
Nor cast me from Thy sight;
Nor let Thy Holy Spirit take
Its everlasting flight.

XXIII.

FROM lowest depths of woe
To God I sent my cry;
Lord, hear my supplicating voice,
And graciously reply.

My soul with patience waits
For Thee, the living Lord;
My hopes are on Thy promise built,
Thy never-failing word.

My longing eyes look out
For Thy enlivening ray,
More duly than the morning watch
To spy the dawning day.

Let Israel trust in God;
No bounds His mercy knows,
The plenteous source and spring from whence
Eternal succour flows:

Whose friendly streams to us
Supplies in want convey;
A healing spring, a spring to cleanse,
And wash our guilt away.

XXIV.

WHEN I survey the wondrous Cross
  On which the Prince of glory died,
My richest gain I count but loss,
  And pour contempt on all my pride.

Forbid it, Lord, that I should boast,
  Save in the death of Christ my God;
All the vain things that charm me most,
  I sacrifice them to His blood.

See from His head, His hands, His feet,
  Sorrow and love flow mingled down!
Did e'er such love and sorrow meet,
  Or thorns compose so rich a crown?

Were the whole realm of nature mine,
  That were a present far too small;
Love so amazing, so divine,
  Demands my soul, my life, my all.

XXV.

JESU, lover of my soul,
  Let me to Thy bosom fly,
While the nearer waters roll,
  While the tempest still is high:
Hide me, O my Saviour, hide,
  Till the storm of life is past;
Safe into the haven guide,
  O receive my soul at last!

Other refuge have I none;
  Hangs my helpless soul on Thee;
Leave, ah! leave me not alone,
  Still support and comfort me:
All my trust on Thee is stayed,
  All my help from Thee I bring;
Cover my defenceless head
  With the shadow of Thy wing.

Plenteous grace with Thee is found,
  Grace to cover all my sin;
Let the healing streams abound,
  Make and keep me pure within;
Thou of life the fountain art,
  Freely let me take of Thee;
Spring Thou up within my heart,
  Rise to all eternity!

XXVI.

ROCK of ages, cleft for me,
Let me hide myself in Thee;
Let the water and the blood,
From Thy riven side which flowed,
Be of sin the double cure,
Cleanse me from its guilt and power.

Nothing in my hand I bring,
Simply to Thy Cross I cling:
Could my tears for ever flow,
Could my zeal no respite know,
All for sin could not atone,
Thou must save, and Thou alone.

While I draw this fleeting breath,
When mine eye-strings break in death,
When I soar through tracts unknown,
See Thee on Thy judgment throne,
Rock of ages, cleft for me,
Let me hide myself in Thee!

XXVII.

COME, let us to the Lord our God
  With contrite hearts return;
Our God is gracious, nor will leave
  The desolate to mourn.

His voice commands the tempest forth,
  And stills the stormy wave;
And, though His arm be strong to smite,
  'Tis also strong to save.

Long hath the night of sorrow reigned;
  The dawn shall bring us light;
God shall appear, and we shall rise
  With gladness in His sight.

Our hearts, if God we seek to know,
  Shall know Him, and rejoice;
His coming like the morn shall be,
  Like morning songs His voice.

As dew upon the tender herb,
  Diffusing fragrance round;
As showers that usher in the spring,
  And cheer the thirsty ground;

So shall His presence bless our souls,
  And shed a joyful light;
That hallowed morn shall chase away
  The sorrows of the night.

XXVIII.

SAVIOUR, when in dust to Thee
Low we bend the adoring knee;
When, repentant, to the skies
Scarce we lift our weeping eyes;
O by all the pains and woe
Suffered once for man below,
Bending from Thy throne on high,
Hear our solemn litany!

By Thy helpless infant years,
By Thy life of want and tears,
By Thy days of sore distress
In the savage wilderness;
By the dread mysterious hour
Of the insulting tempter's power;
Turn, O turn a favouring eye,
Hear our solemn litany!

By the sacred griefs that wept
O'er the grave where Lazarus slept;
By the boding tears that flowed
Over Salem's loved abode;
By the anguished sigh that told
Treachery lurked within Thy fold;
From Thy seat above the sky,
Hear our solemn litany!

By Thine hour of dire despair;
By Thine agony of prayer;
By the cross, the nail, the thorn,
Piercing spear, and torturing scorn;
By the gloom that veiled the skies
O'er the dreadful sacrifice;
Listen to our humble cry,
Hear our solemn litany!

By Thy deep expiring groan;
By the sad sepulchral stone;
By the vault, whose dark abode
Held in vain the rising God;
O from earth to heaven restored,
Mighty re-ascended Lord,
Listen, listen to the cry
Of our solemn litany!

XXIX.

LORD of mercy and of might,
Of mankind the life and light,
Maker, Teacher infinite!
Jesus, hear and save!

Who, when sin's tremendous doom
Gave creation to the tomb,
Didst not scorn the Virgin's womb,
Jesus, hear and save!

Mighty Monarch, Saviour mild,
Humbled to a mortal child,
Captive, beaten, bound, reviled,
Jesus, hear and save!

Throned above celestial things,
Borne aloft on angels' wings,
Lord of lords, and King of kings,
Jesus, hear and save!

Who shalt yet return from high,
Robed in might and majesty,
Hear us, help us when we cry!
Jesus, hear and save!

XXX.

O HELP us, Lord! each hour of need,
  Thy heavenly succour give;
Help us in thought, and word, and deed,
  Each hour on earth we live.

O help us when our spirits bleed
  With contrite anguish sore;
And when our hearts are cold and dead,
  O help us, Lord, the more!

O help us, through the prayer of faith,
  More firmly to believe;
For still, the more the servant hath,
  The more shall he receive.

O help us, Jesus, from on high!
  We know no help but Thee:
O help us so to live and die,
  As Thine in heaven to be!

XXXI.

RIDE on! ride on in majesty!
Hark! all the tribes Hosanna cry;
Thine humble beast pursues his road
With palms and scattered garments strewed.

Ride on! ride on in majesty!
In lowly pomp ride on to die:
O Christ, Thy triumphs now begin
O'er captive death and conquered sin.

Ride on! ride on in majesty!
The wingèd squadrons of the sky
Look down with sad and wondering eyes
To see the approaching sacrifice.

Ride on! ride on in majesty!
Thy last and fiercest strife is nigh:
The Father on His sapphire throne
Expects His own anointed Son.

Ride on! ride on in majesty!
In lowly pomp ride on to die;
Bow Thy meek head to mortal pain;
Then take, O God, Thy power, and reign.

XXXII.

LORD, in this Thy mercy's day,
Ere it pass for aye away,
On our knees we fall and pray.

Holy Jesu, grant us tears,
Fill us with heart-searching fears
Ere that awful doom appears.

Lord, on us Thy Spirit pour,
Kneeling lowly at the door
Ere it close for evermore.

By Thy night of agony,
By Thy supplicating cry,
By Thy willingness to die,

By Thy tears of bitter woe
For Jerusalem below,
Let us not Thy love forego.

Grant us 'neath Thy wings a place,
Lest we lose this day of grace
Ere we shall behold Thy face.

XXXIII.

PRAISE to the Holiest in the height,
  And in the depth be praise;
In all His words most wonderful,
  Most sure in all His ways.

O loving wisdom of our God!
  When all was sin and shame,
  second Adam to the fight
  And to the rescue came.

O wisest love! that flesh and blood,
  Which did in Adam fail,
Should strive afresh against the foe,
  Should strive and should prevail;

And that a higher gift than grace
  Should flesh and blood refine;
God's presence and His very Self,
  And essence all-divine.

O generous love! that He who smote
  In man for man the foe,
The double agony in man
  For man should undergo;

And in the garden secretly,
  And on the cross on high,
Should teach His brethren, and inspire
  To suffer and to die.

Praise to the Holiest in the height,
  And in the depth be praise:
In all His words most wonderful,
  Most sure in all His ways.

EASTER.

XXXIV.

AT the Lamb's high feast we sing
Praise to our victorious King,
Who hath washed us in the tide
Flowing from His piercèd side;
Praise we Him, whose love divine
Gives His sacred Blood for wine,
Gives His Body for the feast,
Christ the Victim, Christ the Priest.

Where the Paschal blood is poured,
Death's dark angel sheathes his sword;
Israel's hosts triumphant go
Through the wave that drowns the foe.
Praise we Christ, whose blood was shed,
Paschal victim, Paschal bread;
With sincerity and love
Eat we manna from above.

Mighty Victim from the sky,
Hell's fierce powers beneath Thee lie;
Thou hast conquered in the fight,
Thou hast brought us life and light;
Now no more can death appal,
Now no more the grave enthral;
Thou hast opened paradise,
And Thy saints in Thee shall rise.

Paschal triumph, Paschal joy,
Only sin can this destroy;
From the death of sin set free
Souls new-born, dear Lord, in Thee.
Hymns of glory, songs of praise,
Father, unto Thee we raise;
Risen Lord, all praise to Thee,
With the Spirit, ever be.

XXXV.

JESUS Christ is risen to-day, Alleluia!
Our triumphant holy day; Alleluia!
Who did once upon the cross Alleluia!
Suffer to redeem our loss; Alleluia!

Hymns of praise then let us sing Alleluia!
Unto Christ our heavenly King, Alleluia!
Who endured the cross and grave, Alleluia!
Sinners to redeem and save; Alleluia!

But the pain which He endured, Alleluia!
Our salvation has procured; Alleluia!
Now above the sky He's King, Alleluia!
Where the angels ever sing Alleluia!

XXXVI.

ALLELUIA!
Finita jam sunt prœlia:
Est parta jam victoria.
Gaudeamus et canamus Alleluia!

Post fata mortis barbara,
Devicit Jesus Tartara;
Applaudamus et psallamus Alleluia!

Surrexit die tertia
Cœlesti clarus gratia:
Insonemus et cantemus Alleluia!

Sunt clausa Stygis ostia,
Et cœli patent atria:
Gaudeamus et canamus Alleluia!

O coronate gloria,
Tua nos morte libera,
Ut vivamus et canamus Alleluia!

XXXVII.

JESUS lives! no longer now
  Can thy terrors, Death, appal us;
Jesus lives! by this we know
  Thou, O Grave, canst not enthral us.
          Alleluia!

Jesus lives! henceforth is death
  But the gate of life immortal;
This shall calm our trembling breath,
  When we pass its gloomy portal.
          Alleluia!

Jesus lives! for us He died:
  Then, alone to Jesus living,
Pure in heart may we abide,
  Glory to our Saviour giving.
          Alleluia!

Jesus lives! our hearts know well
  Naught from us His love shall sever;
Life, nor death, nor powers of hell
  Tear us from His keeping ever.
          Alleluia!

Jesus lives! to Him the throne
  Over all the world is given:
May we go where He is gone,
  Rest and reign with Him in heaven.
          Alleluia!

XXXVIII.

CHRIST the Lord is risen to-day,
Sons of men and angels say;
Raise your joys and triumphs high,
Sing, ye heavens, and earth reply.

Vain the stone, the watch, the seal;
Christ hath burst the gates of hell;
Death in vain forbids His rise;
Christ hath opened Paradise.

Lives again our glorious King;
Where, O Death, is now thy sting?
Once He died, our souls to save;
Where thy victory, O Grave?

Soar we now where Christ has led,
Following our exalted Head;
Made like Him, like Him we rise;
Ours the cross, the grave, the skies.

Hail the Lord of earth and heaven!
Praise to Thee by both be given!
Thee we greet triumphant now;
Hail, the Resurrection Thou!

XXXIX.

JERUSALEM the golden!
With milk and honey blest;
Beneath thy contemplation
Sink heart and voice opprest.

For thee, O dear, dear Country,
Mine eyes their vigils keep;
For very love, beholding
Thy happy name, they weep.

O one, O only mansion!
O Paradise of joy!
Where tears are ever banished,
And smiles have no alloy;

The Lamb is all thy splendour,
The Crucified thy praise;
His laud and benediction
Thy ransomed people raise.

They stand, those halls of Sion,
All jubilant with song,
And bright with many an angel,
And all the martyr throng:

And they who with their Leader
Have conquered in the fight,
For ever and for ever
Are clad in robes of white.

ASCENSION.

XL.

O CHRIST, who hast prepared a place
For us around Thy throne of grace,
We pray Thee, lift our hearts above,
And draw them with the cords of love.

Source of all good, Thou, gracious Lord,
Art our exceeding great reward;
How transient is our present pain!
How boundless our eternal gain!

With open face and joyful heart,
We then shall see Thee as Thou art;
Our love shall never cease to glow,
Our praise shall never cease to flow.

Thy never-failing grace to prove,
A surety of Thine endless love,
Send down Thy Holy Ghost, to be
The raiser of our souls to Thee.

XLI.

HAIL the day that sees Him rise, Alleluia!
Ravished from our wishful eyes, Alleluia!
Christ, awhile to mortals given, Alleluia!
Reascends His native heaven; Alleluia!

There the pompous triumph waits; Alleluia!
Lift your heads, eternal gates! Alleluia!
Conqueror over death and sin, Alleluia!
Take the King of glory in, Alleluia!

See, He lifts His hands above; Alleluia!
See, He shows the prints of love; Alleluia!
Hark, His gracious lips bestow, Alleluia!
Blessings on His Church below; Alleluia!

Him though highest heaven receives, Alleluia!
Yet He loves the earth He leaves; Alleluia!
Though returning to His throne, Alleluia!
Still He calls mankind His own; Alleluia!

Still for us His death He pleads, Alleluia!
Prevalent He intercedes, Alleluia!
Near Himself prepares our place, Alleluia!
Harbinger of human race; Alleluia!

Lord, though parted from our sight, Alleluia!
High above yon azure height, Alleluia!
Grant our hearts may thither rise, Alleluia!
Following Thee beyond the skies; Alleluia!

XLII.

THOU art gone up on high,
  To realms beyond the skies;
And round Thy throne unceasingly
  The songs of praise arise;
But we are lingering here,
  With sin and care oppressed;
Lord, send Thy promised Comforter,
  And lead us to our rest.

Thou art gone up on high;
  But Thou didst first come down,
Through earth's most bitter agony
  To pass unto Thy crown;
And girt with griefs and fears
  Our onward course must be;
But only let this path of tears
  Lead us at last to Thee.

Thou art gone up on high;
  But Thou shalt come again,
With all the bright ones of the sky
  Attendant in Thy train:
Lord, by Thy saving power,
  So make us live and die,
That we may stand in that dread hour
  At Thy right hand on high.

XLIII.

HE is gone—beyond the skies,
A cloud receives Him from our eyes;
Gone beyond the highest height
Of mortal gaze or angels' flight;
Through the veils of time and space,
Passed into the Holiest Place;
All the toil, the sorrow done,
All the battle fought and won.

He is gone—we heard Him say,
"Good that I should go away:"
Gone is that dear form and face,
But not gone His present grace;
Though Himself no more we see,
Comfortless we cannot be,
For His Spirit still is ours,
Quickening, freshening all our powers.

He is gone—but we once more
Shall behold Him as before;
In the heaven of heavens the same,
As on earth He went and came.
In the many mansions there,
Place for us will He prepare:
In that world, unseen, unknown,
He and we may yet be one.

He is gone—but, not in vain,
Wait, until He comes again;
He is risen, He is not here,
Far above this earthly sphere;
Evermore in heart and mind,
Where our peace in Him we find,
To our own eternal Friend,
Thitherward let us ascend.

WHITSUNTIDE.

XLIV.

VENI, Creator Spiritus,
Mentes tuorum visita,
Imple superna gratia
Quæ tu creâsti pectora.

Qui Paraclitus diceris,
Altissimi donum Dei,
Fons vivus, ignis, caritas,
Et spiritalis unctio.

Tu septiformis munere,
Dextræ Dei tu digitus,
Tu rite promissum Patris,
Sermone ditans guttura.

Accende lumen sensibus,
Infunde amorem cordibus,
Infirma nostri corporis
Virtute firmans perpeti.

Hostem repellas longius,
Pacemque dones protinus,
Ductore sic Te prævio
Vitemus omne noxium.

Da gaudiorum præmia,
Da gratiarum munera,
Dissolve litis vincula,
Adstringe pacis fœdera.

Per te sciamus, da, Patrem,
Noscamus atque Filium,
Te utriusque Spiritum
Credamus omni tempore.

Sit laus Patri cum Filio,
Sancto simul Paraclito,
Nobisque mittat Filius
Charisma Sancti Spiritûs.

XLV.

VENI, Sancte Spiritus,
Et emitte cœlitus
Lucis Tuæ radium.

Veni, pater pauperum,
Veni, dator munerum,
Veni, lumen cordium:

Consolator optime,
Dulcis hospes animæ,
Dulce refrigerium:

In labore requies,
In æstu temperies,
In fletu solatium.

O Lux beatissima,
Reple cordis intima
Tuorum fidelium.

Sine Tuo numine
Nihil est in homine,
Nihil est innoxium.

Lava quod est sordidum,
Riga quod est aridum,
Sana quod est saucium:

Flecte quod est rigidum,
Fove quod est frigidum,
Rege quod est devium.

Da Tuis fidelibus
In Te confidentibus
Sacrum septenarium;

Da virtutis meritum,
Da salutis exitum,
Da perenne gaudium.

XLVI.

COME, Holy Ghost, our souls inspire,
And lighten with celestial fire;
Thou the anointing Spirit art,
Who dost Thy sevenfold gifts impart:

Thy blessed unction from above
Is comfort, life, and fire of love;
Enable with perpetual light
The dulness of our blinded sight:

Anoint and cheer our soilèd face
With the abundance of Thy grace;
Keep far our foes, give peace at home;
Where Thou art guide, no ill can come.

Teach us to know the Father, Son,
And Thee, of Both, to be but One;
That, through the ages all along,
This may be our endless song,
  Praise to Thy eternal merit,
  Father, Son, and Holy Spirit.

XLVII.

SPIRIT of mercy, truth, and love,
O shed Thine influence from above;
And still from age to age convey
The wonders of this sacred day.

In every clime, by every tongue,
Be God's surpassing glory sung;
Let all the listening earth be taught
The wonders by our Saviour wrought.

Unfailing Comfort, heavenly Guide,
Still o'er Thy holy Church preside;
Still let mankind Thy blessings prove,
Spirit of mercy, truth, and love.

XLVIII.

WHEN God of old came down from heaven,
  In power and wrath He came;
Before His feet the clouds were riven,
  Half darkness and half flame:

But when He came the second time,
  He came in power and love;
Softer than gale at morning prime
  Hovered His holy Dove.

The fires, that rushed on Sinai down
  In sudden torrents dread,
Now gently light, a glorious crown,
  On every sainted head.

And as on Israel's awe-struck ear
  The voice exceeding loud,
The trump, that angels quake to hear,
  Thrilled from the deep, dark cloud;

So, when the Spirit of our God
  Came down His flock to find,
A voice from heaven was heard abroad,
  A rushing, mighty wind.

It fills the Church of God; it fills
  The sinful world around;
Only in stubborn hearts and wills
  No place for it is found.

Come, Lord, come, Wisdom, Love, and Power,
  Open our ears to hear;
Let us not miss the accepted hour;
  Save, Lord, by love or fear.

XLIX.

OUR blest Redeemer, ere He breathed
His tender last farewell,
A Guide, a Comforter, bequeathed
With us to dwell.

He came sweet influence to impart,
A gracious willing guest,
While He can find one humble heart
Wherein to rest.

And His that gentle voice we hear,
Soft as the breath of even,
That checks each thought, that calms each fear,
And speaks of heaven.

And every virtue we possess,
And every conquest won,
And every thought of holiness,
Are His alone.

Spirit of purity and grace,
Our weakness, pitying, see:
O make our hearts Thy dwelling-place,
And worthier Thee.

O praise the Father; praise the Son;
Blest Spirit, praise to Thee;
All praise to God, the Three in One,
The One in Three.

TRINITY SUNDAY.

L.

GOD, the Father, Son, and Spirit,
  Three in One, and One in Three,
Thine united glories merit
  Thanks and praise continually:

Praise to Thee and adoration
  On Thy festival be done,
For the blessed Incarnation
  Of the Co-eternal Son;

More than all, be praise unending
  Paid throughout Thy Church to Thee
For the majesty transcending
  Of Thy Triune Deity:

Sun of splendour never waning,
  Fount of sweetness never dry,
Staff of comfort all-sustaining,
  Ever-blessed Trinity!

LI.

HOLY, holy, holy, Lord God Almighty!
 Early in the morning our song shall rise to Thee;
Holy, holy, holy! merciful and mighty!
 God in Three Persons, blessed Trinity!

Holy, holy, holy! all the saints adore Thee,
 Casting down their golden crowns around the glassy
 sea;
Cherubim and seraphim falling down before Thee,
 Which wert, and art, and evermore shalt be.

Holy, holy, holy! though the darkness hide Thee,
 Though the eye of sinful man Thy glory may not see,
Only Thou art holy; there is none beside Thee,
 Perfect in power, in love and purity.

Holy, holy, holy, Lord God Almighty!
 All Thy works shall praise Thy name in earth and
 sky and sea;
Holy, holy, holy! merciful and mighty!
 God in Three Persons, blessed Trinity!

LII.

O GOD of life, whose power benign
Doth o'er the world in mercy shine,
Accept our praise, for we are Thine.

O Father, uncreated Lord,
Be Thou in every land adored,
Be Thou with faith by all implored.

O Son of God, for sinners slain,
We bless Thee, Lord, whose dying pain
For us did endless life regain.

O Holy Ghost, whose guardian care
Doth us for heavenly joys prepare,
May we in Thy communion share.

O Holy Blessed Trinity,
With faith we sinners bow to Thee;
In us, O God, exalted be!

SAINTS' DAYS.

LIII.

WHO are these like stars appearing,
These, before God's throne who stand?
Each a golden crown is wearing,
Who are all this glorious band?
Alleluia! hark, they sing,
Praising loud their heavenly King.

Who are these in dazzling brightness,
Clothed in God's own righteousness?
These, whose robes of purest whiteness
Shall their lustre still possess,
Still untouched by time's rude hand,—
Whence comes all this glorious band?

These are they who have contended
For their Saviour's honour long,
Wrestling on till life was ended,
Following not the sinful throng;
These, who well the fight sustained,
Triumph by the Lamb have gained.

These are they whose hearts were riven,
  Sore with woe and anguish tried,
Who in prayer full oft have striven
  With the God they glorified;
    Now, their painful conflict o'er,
    God has bid them weep no more.

These, the Almighty contemplating,
  Did as priests before Him stand,
Soul and body always waiting
  Day and night at His command:
    Now in God's most holy place
    Blest they stand before His face.

LIV.

HOW bright these glorious spirits shine!
  Whence all their white array?
How came they to the blissful seats
  Of everlasting day?

Lo! these are they from sufferings great
  Who came to realms of light,
And in the blood of Christ have washed
  Those robes which shine so bright.

Now with triumphal palms they stand
  Before the throne on high,
And serve the God they love, amidst
  The glories of the sky.

His presence fills each heart with joy,
  Tunes every mouth to sing;
By day, by night, the sacred courts
  With glad Hosannas ring.

Hunger and thirst are felt no more,
  Nor suns with scorching ray;
God is their sun, whose cheering beams
  Diffuse eternal day.

The Lamb, which dwells amidst the throne,
  Shall o'er them still preside,
Feed them with nourishment divine,
  And all their footsteps guide.

To pastures green He'll lead His flock,
  Where living streams appear;
And God the Lord from every eye
  Shall wipe off every tear.

LV.

THE Son of God goes forth to war,
  A kingly crown to gain;
His blood-red banner streams afar:
  Who follows in His train?

Who best can drink His cup of woe,
  Triumphant over pain,
Who patient bears His cross below,
  He follows in His train.

The martyr first, whose eagle eye
  Could pierce beyond the grave;
Who saw his Master in the sky,
  And called on Him to save.

Like Him, with pardon on his tongue,
  In midst of mortal pain,
He prayed for them that did the wrong:
  Who follows in his train?

A glorious band, the chosen few,
  On whom the Spirit came;
Twelve valiant saints, their hope they knew,
  And mocked the cross and flame.

They met the tyrant's brandished steel,
  The lion's gory mane;
They bowed their necks the death to feel;
  Who follows in their train?

A noble army, men and boys,
The matron and the maid,
Around the Saviour's throne rejoice,
In robes of light arrayed.

They climbed the steep ascent of heaven,
Through peril, toil, and pain:
O God, to us may grace be given
To follow in their train!

LVI.

COME, let us join our friends above,
  That have obtained the prize,
And on the eagle-wings of love
  To joy celestial rise:
Let all the saints terrestrial sing
  With those to glory gone;
For all the servants of our King,
  In earth and heaven, are one.

One family, we dwell in Him,
  One Church, above, beneath;
Though now divided by the stream,
  The narrow stream of death:
One army of the living God,
  To His command we bow;
Part of His host have crossed the flood,
  And part are crossing now.

Our spirits too shall quickly join,
  Like theirs with glory crowned,
And shout to see our Captain's sign,
  To hear His trumpet sound.
O that we now might grasp our Guide!
  O that the word were given!
Come, Lord of hosts! the waves divide,
  And land us all in heaven!

HOLY COMMUNION.

LVII.

LAUDA, Sion, Salvatorem,
Lauda Ducem et Pastorem
In hymnis et canticis;
Quantum potes, tantum aude,
Quia major omni laude,
Nec laudare sufficis.

Laudis thema specialis,
Panis vivus et vitalis
Hodie proponitur,
Quem in sacræ mensa cœnæ
Turbæ fratrum duodenæ
Datum non ambigitur.

Bone Pastor, Panis vere,
Jesu, nostri miserere;
Tu nos pasce, nos tuere,
Tu nos bona fac videre
In terra viventium:
Tu, qui cuncta scis et vales,
Qui nos pascis hic mortales,
Tuos ibi commensales,
Cohæredes et sodales
Fac sanctorum civium.

LVIII.

MY God, and is Thy table spread?
  And does Thy cup with love o'erflow?
Thither be all Thy children led,
  And let them all its sweetness know.

Hail, sacred feast, which Jesus makes,
  Rich banquet of His Flesh and Blood!
Thrice happy he, who here partakes
  That sacred stream, that heavenly food!

Why are its dainties all in vain
  Before unwilling hearts displayed?
Was not for you the Victim slain?
  Are you forbid the children's bread?

O let Thy table honoured be,
  And furnished well with joyful guests;
And may each soul salvation see,
  That here its sacred pledges tastes.

Let crowds approach, with hearts prepared;
  With hearts inflamed let all attend;
Nor, when we leave our Father's board,
  The pleasure or the profit end.

Revive Thy dying churches, Lord!
  And bid our drooping graces live;
And more, that energy afford,
  A Saviour's love alone can give.

LIX.

BREAD of heaven, on Thee we feed,
For Thy Flesh is meat indeed;
Ever may our souls be fed
With this true and living bread;
Day by day with strength supplied
Through the life of Him who died.

Vine of heaven, Thy Blood supplies
This blest cup of sacrifice;
Lord, Thy wounds our healing give,
To Thy cross we look and live:
Jesus, may we ever be
Grafted, rooted, built in Thee.

LX.

O GOD, unseen, yet ever near,
  Thy presence may we feel;
And thus, inspired with holy fear,
  Before Thine altar kneel.

Here may Thy faithful people know
  The blessings of Thy love;
The streams that through the desert flow,
  The manna from above.

We come, obedient to Thy word,
  To feast on heavenly food;
Our meat, the Body of the Lord;
  Our drink, His precious Blood.

Thus would we all Thy words obey,
  For we, O God, are Thine;
And go rejoicing on our way,
  Renewed with strength divine.

FOR GENERAL USE.

LXI.

ALES diei nuntius
Lucem propinquam præcinit;
Nos excitator mentium
Jam Christus ad vitam vocat.

"Auferte," clamat, "lectulos
Ægros, soporos, desides;
Castique, recti, sobrii
Vigilate; jam sum proximus."

Jesum ciamus vocibus
Flentes, precantes, sobrii:
Intenta supplicatio
Dormire cor mundum vetat.

Tu, Christe, somnum disjice,
Tu rumpe noctis vincula:
Tu solve peccatum vetus,
Novumque lumen ingere.

Deo Patri sit gloria,
Ejusque soli Filio,
Sancto simul cum Spiritu
Nunc et per omne sæculum.

LXII.

NOX et tenebræ et nubila
Confusa mundi et turbida,—
Lux intrat, albescit polus,
Christus venit,—discedite.

Caligo terræ scinditur,
Percussa solis spiculo,
Rebusque jam color redit
Vultu nitentis sideris.

Te, Christe, solum novimus,
Te mente pura et simplici
Flendo et canendo quæsumus:
Intende nostris sensibus.

Sunt multa fucis illita
Quæ luce purgentur tua;
Tu, Rex, Eoi sideris
Vultu sereno illumina.

Deo Patri sit gloria,
Ejusque soli Filio,
Cum Spiritu Paraclito,
Nunc et per omne sæculum.

LXIII.

JAM lucis orto sidere
Deum precemur supplices,
Ut in diurnis actibus
Nos servet a nocentibus.

Linguam refrænans temperet,
Ne litis horror insonet;
Visum fovendo contegat,
Ne vanitates hauriat.

Sint pura cordis intima,
Absistat et vecordia;
Carnis terat superbiam
Potûs cibique parcitas:

Ut cum dies abscesserit,
Noctemque sors reduxerit,
Mundi per abstinentiam
Ipsi canamus gloriam.

Deo Patri sit gloria,
Ejusque soli Filio,
Cum Spiritu Paraclito,
Nunc et per omne sæculum.

LXIV.

AWAKE, my soul, and with the sun
Thy daily stage of duty run;
Shake off dull sloth, and joyful rise
To pay thy morning sacrifice.

Thy precious time mis-spent redeem;
Each present day thy last esteem;
Improve thy talent with due care;
For the great day thyself prepare.

In conversation be sincere;
Keep conscience as the noontide clear;
Think how all-seeing God thy ways
And all thy secret thoughts surveys.

By influence of the light divine
Let thy own light to others shine;
Reflect all heaven's propitious rays,
In ardent love and cheerful praise.

Praise God, from whom all blessings flow;
Praise Him, all creatures here below;
Praise Him above, ye heavenly host;
Praise Father, Son, and Holy Ghost.

LXV.

WAKE and lift up thyself, my heart,
And with the angels bear thy part,
Who, all night long, unwearied sing
High praise to the eternal King.

All praise to Thee, who safe hast kept,
And hast refreshed me while I slept;
Grant, Lord, when I from death shall wake,
I may of endless light partake.

Lord, I my vows to Thee renew;
Disperse my sins as morning dew;
Guard my first springs of thought and will,
And with Thyself my spirit fill.

Direct, control, suggest, this day,
All I design, or do, or say;
That all my powers, with all their might,
In Thy sole glory may unite.

Praise God, from whom all blessings flow;
Praise Him, all creatures here below;
Praise Him above, ye heavenly host;
Praise Father, Son, and Holy Ghost.

LXVI.

CHRIST, whose glory fills the skies,
  Christ, the true, the only Light,
Sun of righteousness, arise,
  Triumph o'er the shades of night;
Day-spring from on high, be near;
Day-star, in my heart appear.

Dark and cheerless is the morn
  Unaccompanied by Thee;
Joyless is the day's return,
  Till Thy mercy's beams I see;
Till they inward light impart,
Glad my eyes, and warm my heart.

Visit then this soul of mine,
  Pierce the gloom of sin and grief;
Fill me, Radiancy divine,
  Scatter all my unbelief;
More and more Thyself display,
Shining to the perfect day.

LXVII.

BEHOLD, the morning sun
Begins his glorious way;
His beams through all the nations run,
And life and light convey.

But where the Gospel comes,
It spreads diviner light,
It calls dead sinners from their tombs,
And gives the blind their sight.

How perfect is Thy word,
And all Thy judgments just!
For ever sure Thy promise, Lord;
And men securely trust.

While with my heart and tongue
I spread Thy praise abroad,
Accept the worship and the song,
My Saviour and my God!

LXVIII.

O TIMELY happy, timely wise,
Hearts that with rising morn arise!
Eyes that the beam celestial view,
Which evermore makes all things new!

New every morning is the love
Our wakening and uprising prove,
Through sleep and darkness safely brought,
Restored to life, and power, and thought.

New mercies, each returning day,
Hover around us while we pray;
New perils past, new sins forgiven,
New thoughts of God, new hopes of heaven.

If, on our daily course, our mind
Be set to hallow all we find,
New treasures still, of countless price,
God will provide for sacrifice.

Seek we no more: content with these,
Let present rapture, comfort, ease,
As Heaven shall bid them, come and go;
The secret this of rest below.

Only, O Lord, in Thy dear love
Fit us for perfect rest above;
And help us, this and every day,
To live more nearly as we pray!

LXIX.

COME, Holy Ghost, who ever one
Art with the Father and the Son,
Come, Holy Ghost, our souls possess
With Thy full flood of holiness.

Let flesh, and heart, and lips, and mind,
Sound forth our witness to mankind;
And love light up our mortal frame,
Till others catch the living flame.

Now to the Father, to the Son,
And to the Spirit, Three in One,
Be praise and thanks and glory given
By men on earth, by saints in heaven.

LXX.

O GOD, the Lord of place and time,
  Who orderest all things prudently,
Brightening with beams the opening prime,
  And burning in the midday sky:

Quench Thou the fires of hate and strife,
  The wasting fever of the heart;
From perils guard our feeble life,
  And to our souls Thy peace impart.

Grant this, O Father, Only Son,
  And Holy Spirit, God of grace,
To whom all glory, Three in One,
  Be given in every time and place.

LXXI.

AS now the sun's declining rays
  Towards the eve descend,
E'en so our years are sinking down
  To their appointed end.

Lord, on the Cross Thine arms were stretched,
  To draw us to the sky:
O grant us then that Cross to love,
  And in those arms to die.

All glory to the Father be,
  All glory to the Son,
All glory, Holy Ghost, to Thee,
  While endless ages run.

LXXII.

LIGHT of gladness, Beam divine
From the glory's inmost shrine,
Where in His immortal rest
Reigns Thy Father ever-blest;

Jesus Christ, our hymn receive;
Sunset brings the lights of eve,
Bids us praise the Father, Son,
And the Spirit, Three in One.

Night and day for Thee is meet
Holy voices' anthem sweet,
Ringing through the world abroad,
'Hail, life-giving Son of God!'

LXXIII.

ALL praise to Thee, my God, this night,
For all the blessings of the light;
Keep me, O keep me, King of kings,
Beneath Thine own Almighty wings!

Forgive me, Lord, for Thy dear Son,
The ill that I this day have done;
That with the world, myself, and Thee,
I, ere I sleep, at peace may be.

Teach me to live, that I may dread
The grave as little as my bed;
To die, that this vile body may
Rise glorious at the awful day.

O may my soul on Thee repose,
And may sweet sleep mine eyelids close;
Sleep, that may me more vig'rous make
To serve my God when I awake.

When in the night I sleepless lie,
My soul with heavenly thoughts supply;
Let no ill dreams disturb my rest,
No powers of darkness me molest.

Praise God, from whom all blessings flow;
Praise Him, all creatures here below;
Praise Him above, ye heavenly host;
Praise Father, Son, and Holy Ghost.

LXXIV.

GOD, who madest earth and heaven,
    Darkness and light;
Who the day for toil hast given,
    For rest the night;
May Thine angel-guards defend us,
Slumber sweet Thy mercy send us,
Holy dreams and hopes attend us,
    This livelong night.

Guard us waking, guard us sleeping,
    And, when we die,
May we in Thy mighty keeping
    All peaceful lie:
When the last dread call shall wake us,
Do not Thou, our God, forsake us,
But to reign in glory take us
    With Thee on high.

LXXV.

SUN of my soul, Thou Saviour dear,
It is not night if Thou be near:
O may no earth-born cloud arise
To hide Thee from Thy servant's eyes.

When the soft dews of kindly sleep
My wearied eyelids gently steep,
Be my last thought, how sweet to rest
For ever on my Saviour's breast.

Abide with me from morn till eve,
For without Thee I cannot live;
Abide with me when night is nigh,
For without Thee I dare not die.

If some poor wandering child of Thine
Have spurned, to-day, the voice divine,
Now, Lord, the gracious work begin;
Let him no more lie down in sin.

Watch by the sick; enrich the poor
With blessings from Thy boundless store;
Be every mourner's sleep to-night,
Like infant's slumbers, pure and light.

Come near and bless us when we wake,
Ere through the world our way we take;
Till in the ocean of Thy love
We lose ourselves in heaven above.

LXXVI.

ABIDE with me; fast falls the eventide;
The darkness deepens; Lord, with me abide;
When other helpers fail, and comforts flee,
Help of the helpless, O abide with me.

Swift to its close ebbs out life's little day;
Earth's joys grow dim, its glories pass away;
Change and decay in all around I see;
O Thou who changest not, abide with me.

Thou on my head in early youth didst smile;
And, though rebellious and perverse meanwhile,
Thou hast not left me, oft as I left Thee:
On to the close, O Lord, abide with me.

I need Thy presence every passing hour;
What but Thy grace can foil the tempter's power?
Who like Thyself my guide and stay can be?
Through cloud and sunshine, Lord, abide with me.

I fear no foe with Thee at hand to bless;
Ills have no weight, and tears no bitterness;
Where is death's sting? where, grave, thy victory?
I triumph still, if Thou abide with me.

Hold Thou Thy cross before my closing eyes;
Shine through the gloom, and point me to the skies;
Heaven's morning breaks, and earth's vain shadows flee;
In life, in death, O Lord, abide with me.

LXXVII.

ART thou weary, art thou languid,
Art thou sore distrest?
"Come to Me, saith One, and coming
Be at rest!"

Hath He marks to lead me to Him,
If He be my guide?
"In His feet and hands are wound-prints
And His side."

Is there diadem, as Monarch,
That His brow adorns?
"Yea, a crown, in very surety,
But of thorns."

If I find Him, if I follow,
What His guerdon here?
"Many a sorrow, many a labour,
Many a tear."

If I still hold closely to Him,
What hath He at last?
"Sorrow vanquished, labour ended,
Jordan past."

If I ask Him to receive me,
Will He say me nay?
"Not till earth, and not till heaven
Pass away."

Finding, following, keeping, struggling,
Is He sure to bless?
"Angels, martyrs, prophets, virgins
Answer, Yes!"

LXXVIII.

SWEET Saviour, bless us ere we go ;
  Thy word into our minds instil ;
And make our lukewarm hearts to glow
  With lowly love and fervent will :
Through life's long day and death's dark night,
O gentle Jesus, be our light.

The day is gone, its hours have run,
  And Thou hast taken count of all,
The scanty triumphs grace hath won,
  The broken vow, the frequent fall :
Through life's long day and death's dark night,
O gentle Jesus, be our light.

Grant us, dear Lord, from evil ways
  True absolution and release ;
And bless us, more than in past days,
  With purity and inward peace :
Through life's long day and death's dark night,
O gentle Jesus, be our light.

Do more than pardon ; give us joy,
  Sweet fear, and sober liberty,
And simple hearts without alloy
  That only long to be like Thee :
Through life's long day and death's dark night,
O gentle Jesus, be our light.

Labour is sweet, for Thou hast toiled;
  And care is light, for Thou hast cared;
Let not our works by strife be soiled,
  Nor in unsimple ways ensnared:
Through life's long day and death's dark night,
O gentle Jesus, be our light.

For all we love, the poor, the sad,
  The sinful, unto Thee we call;
O let Thy mercy make us glad!
  Thou art our Jesus, and our All:
Through life's long day and death's dark night,
O gentle Jesus, be our light.

LXXIX.

BRIEF life is here our portion;
  Brief sorrow, short-lived care;
The life that knows no ending,
  The tearless life, is *there*.

O happy retribution!
  Short toil, eternal rest;
For mortals and for sinners
  A mansion with the blest.

And now we fight the battle,
  But then shall wear the crown
Of full and everlasting
  And passionless renown;

And now we watch and struggle,
  And now we live in hope,
And Sion in her anguish
  With Babylon must cope;

But He whom now we trust in
  Shall then be seen and known;
And they that know and see Him
  Shall have Him for their own.

The morning shall awaken,
  The shadows shall decay,
And each true-hearted servant
  Shall shine as doth the day;

Yes! God, my King and portion,
  In fulness of His grace,
Shall we behold for ever,
  And worship face to face.

LXXX.

THE Lord descended from above,
  And bowed the heavens most high;
And underneath His feet He cast
  The darkness of the sky;

On cherubs and on cherubims
  Full royally He rode,
And on the wings of mighty winds
  Came flying all abroad.

Unspotted are the ways of God,
  His word is purely tried;
He is a sure defence to such
  As in His faith abide.

For who is God, except the Lord?
  For other there is none:
Or else who is omnipotent,
  Saving our God alone?

LXXXI.

ALL people that on earth do dwell,
  Sing to the Lord with cheerful voice;
Him serve with fear, His praise forth tell,
  Come ye before Him and rejoice.

The Lord, ye know, is God indeed;
  Without our aid He did us make:
We are His flock, He doth us feed,
  And for His sheep He doth us take.

O enter then His gates with praise,
  Approach with joy His courts unto;
Praise, laud, and bless His Name always,
  For it is seemly so to do.

For why? the Lord our God is good,
  His mercy is for ever sure;
His truth at all times firmly stood,
  And shall from age to age endure.

LXXXII.

COMMIT thou all thy griefs
And ways into His hands,
To His sure truth and tender care,
Who earth and heaven commands.

Who points the clouds their course,
Whom winds and seas obey,
He shall direct thy wandering feet,
He shall prepare thy way.

Thou on the Lord rely;
So safe shalt thou go on;
Fix on His work thy stedfast eye,
So shall thy work be done.

Thou seest our weakness, Lord!
Our hearts are known to Thee:
O lift Thou up the sinking hand,
Confirm the feeble knee!

Let us, in life, in death,
Thy stedfast truth declare,
And publish, with our latest breath,
Thy love and guardian care.

LXXXIII.

O THOU, to whom all creatures bow
  Within this earthly frame,
Through all the world how great art Thou!
  How glorious is Thy name!

In heaven Thy wondrous acts are sung,
  Nor fully reckoned there;
And yet Thou mak'st the infant tongue
  Thy boundless praise declare.

Through Thee the weak confound the strong,
  And crush their haughty foes;
And so Thou quell'st the wicked throng,
  That Thee and Thine oppose.

What's man, (say I,) that, Lord, Thou lov'st
  To keep him in Thy mind?
Or what his offspring, that Thou prov'st
  To them so wondrous kind?

They jointly own His powerful sway;
  The beasts that prey or graze;
The bird that wings its airy way;
  The fish that cuts the seas.

O Thou to whom all creatures bow
  Within this earthly frame,
Through all the world how great art Thou!
  How glorious is Thy name!

LXXXIV.

TO bless Thy chosen race,
  In mercy, Lord, incline;
And cause the brightness of Thy face
  On all Thy saints to shine:
That so Thy wondrous way
  May through the world be known,
Whilst distant lands their tribute pay,
  And Thy salvation own.

Let differing nations join
  To celebrate Thy fame;
Let all the world, O Lord, combine
  To praise Thy glorious name.
O let them shout and sing
  With joy and pious mirth,
For Thou, the righteous Judge and King,
  Shalt govern all the earth.

LXXXV.

O GOD of hosts, the mighty Lord,
  How lovely is the place
Where Thou, enthroned in glory, show'st
  The brightness of Thy face!

My longing soul faints with desire
  To view Thy blest abode;
My panting heart and flesh cry out
  For Thee, the living God.

O Lord of hosts, my King and God,
  How highly blest are they
Who in Thy temple always dwell,
  And there Thy praise display!

Thrice happy they, whose choice has Thee
  Their sure protection made;
Who long to tread the sacred ways
  That to Thy dwelling lead!

For God, who is our sun and shield,
  Will grace and glory give;
And no good thing will He withhold
  From them that justly live.

LXXXVI.

WITH glory clad, with strength arrayed,
The Lord, that o'er all nature reigns,
The world's foundations strongly laid,
And the vast fabric still sustains.
How surely 'stablished is Thy throne,
Which shall no change or period see!
For Thou, O Lord, and Thou alone,
Art God from all eternity.

The floods, O Lord, lift up their voice,
And toss the troubled waves on high;
But God above can still their noise,
And make the angry sea comply.
Thy promise, Lord, is ever sure;
And they that in Thy house would dwell,
That happy station to secure,
Must still in holiness excel.

LXXXVII.

O COME, loud anthems let us sing,
Loud thanks to our Almighty King;
For we our voices high should raise
When our salvation's Rock we praise.

Into His presence let us haste,
To thank Him for His favours past;
To Him address, in joyful songs,
The praise that to His name belongs.

The depths of earth are in His hand,
Her secret wealth at His command;
The strength of hills that reach the skies
Subjected to His empire lies.

The rolling ocean's vast abyss
By the same sov'reign right is His;
'Tis moved by His Almighty hand,
That formed and fixed the solid land.

O let us to His courts repair,
And bow with adoration there;
Down on our knees devoutly all
Before the Lord our Maker fall.

LXXXVIII.

MY soul, inspired with sacred love,
  God's holy name for ever bless;
Of all His favours mindful prove,
  And still thy grateful thanks express.

'Tis He that all thy sins forgives,
  And after sickness makes thee sound;
From danger He thy life retrieves,
  By Him with grace and mercy crowned.

God will not always harshly chide,
  But with His anger quickly part;
And loves His punishments to guide
  More by His love than our desert.

As high as heaven its arch extends
  Above this little spot of clay,
So much His boundless love transcends
  The small respects that we can pay.

As far as 'tis from east to west,
  So far has He our sins removed,
Who with a Father's tender breast
  Has such as fear Him always loved.

LXXXIX.

THOU, Lord, by strictest search hast known
My rising up and lying down;
My secret thoughts are known to Thee,
Known long before conceived by me.

Thine eye my bed and path surveys,
My public haunts and private ways;
Thou know'st what 'tis my lips would vent,
My yet unuttered words' intent.

Surrounded by Thy power I stand,
On every side I find Thy hand:
O skill, for human reach too high!
Too dazzling bright for mortal eye!

Search, try, O God, my thoughts and heart,
If mischief lurks in any part;
Correct me where I go astray,
And guide me in Thy perfect way.

XC.

YE boundless realms of joy,
  Exalt your Maker's fame,
His praise your song employ
  Above the starry frame;
    Your voices raise,
      Ye cherubim
      And seraphim,
    To sing His praise.

Thou moon, that rul'st the night,
  And sun, that guid'st the day:
Ye glittering stars of light,
  To Him your homage pay;
    His praise declare,
      Ye heavens above,
      And clouds that move
    In liquid air.

Let them adore the Lord,
  And praise His holy Name,
By whose Almighty word
  They all from nothing came;
    And all shall last
      From changes free,
      His firm decree
    Stands ever fast.

To God the Father, Son,
  And Spirit, ever blest,
Eternal Three in One,
  All worship be addrest;
    As heretofore
      It was, is now,
      And shall be so
    For evermore.

XCI.

THE spacious firmament on high,
With all the blue ethereal sky,
And spangled heavens, a shining frame,
Their great Original proclaim.
The unwearied sun, from day to day,
Does his Creator's power display,
And publishes to every land
The work of an Almighty hand.

Soon as the evening shades prevail,
The moon takes up the wondrous tale,
And nightly to the listening earth
Repeats the story of her birth;
Whilst all the stars that round her burn,
And all the planets in their turn,
Confirm the tidings, as they roll,
And spread the truth from pole to pole.

What, though in solemn silence all
Move round the dark terrestrial ball?
What, though no real voice or sound
Amidst their radiant orbs be found?
In reason's ear they all rejoice,
And utter forth a glorious voice,
For ever singing, as they shine,
"The hand that made us is Divine."

XCII.

THE Lord my pasture shall prepare,
And feed me with a Shepherd's care;
His presence shall my wants supply,
And guard me with a watchful eye;
My noon-day walks He shall attend,
And all my midnight hours defend.

When in the sultry glebe I faint,
Or on the thirsty mountain pant,
To fertile vales and dewy meads
My weary, wandering steps He leads,
Where peaceful rivers, soft and slow,
Amid the verdant landscape flow.

Though in the paths of death I tread,
With gloomy horrors overspread,
My stedfast heart shall fear no ill,
For Thou, O Lord, art with me still;
Thy friendly crook shall give me aid,
And guide me through the dreadful shade.

XCIII.

WHEN all Thy mercies, O my God,
My rising soul surveys,
Transported with the view, I'm lost
In wonder, love, and praise.

Thy Providence my life sustained,
And all my wants redressed,
When in the silent womb I lay,
And hung upon the breast.

Unnumbered comforts to my soul
Thy tender care bestowed,
Before my infant heart conceived
From whence these comforts flowed.

When in the slippery paths of youth
With heedless steps I ran,
Thine arm, unseen, conveyed me safe,
And led me up to man.

Ten thousand thousand precious gifts
My daily thanks employ;
Nor is the least a cheerful heart
That tastes those gifts with joy.

Through every period of my life
Thy goodness I'll pursue;
And after death, in distant worlds,
The glorious theme renew.

XCIV.

O GENTES omnes undique,
  Laudate Dominum;
Illum laudate, populi,
  Per orbis ambitum.

Nam ingens est hominibus
  Illius bonitas,
Et in æterna sæcula
  Jehovæ veritas.

Sit laus Triuni Domino,
  Honor et gloria,
Ab universo populo,
  Per cuncta sæcula.

XCV.

TE de profundis, summe Rex,
Jehovah! supplex invoco;
Intende voci supplicis:
Ad Te precantem suspice.

Delicta si peccantium
Severus observaveris,
Quis sustinebit impius?
Piusve quis non deficit?

Tibi paterna lenitas:
Hinc Te veremur filii:
Te sustinemur unico
A lucis orto sidere.

Fiduciam tantamque spem
In Te reponit Israel,
Tuo, Deus, qui sanguine
Peccata mundi diluis.

Deo Patri sit gloria,
Ejusque soli Filio,
Sanctissimo cum Spiritu
In sæculorum sæcula.

XCVI.

BEFORE Jehovah's awful throne,
  Ye nations, bow with sacred joy;
Know that the Lord is God alone,
  He can create, and He destroy.

His sovereign power, without our aid,
  Made us of clay, and formed us men;
And when like wandering sheep we strayed,
  He brought us to His fold again.

We'll crowd Thy gates with thankful songs,
  High as the heavens our voices raise;
And earth, with her ten thousand tongues,
  Shall fill Thy courts with sounding praise.

Wide as the world is Thy command,
  Vast as eternity Thy love;
Firm as a rock Thy truth must stand,
  When rolling years shall cease to move.

XCVII.

OUR God, our help in ages past,
  Our hope for years to come,
Our shelter from the stormy blast,
  And our eternal home:

Under the shadow of Thy throne
  Thy saints have dwelt secure;
Sufficient is Thine arm alone,
  And our defence is sure.

Before the hills in order stood,
  Or earth received her frame,
From everlasting Thou art God,
  To endless years the same.

A thousand ages in Thy sight
  Are like an evening gone;
Short as the watch that ends the night
  Before the rising sun.

The busy tribes of flesh and blood,
  With all their lives and cares,
Are carried downwards by Thy flood,
  And lost in following years.

Time, like an ever-rolling stream,
  Bears all its sons away;
They fly forgotten, as a dream
  Dies at the opening day.

Our God, our help in ages past,
  Our hope for years to come;
Be Thou our guard while troubles last,
  And our eternal home!

XCVIII.

UP to the hills I lift mine eyes,
The eternal hills beyond the skies;
Thence all her help my soul derives,
There my Almighty Refuge lives.

He lives, the everlasting God,
That built the world, that spread the flood;
The heavens with all their hosts He made,
And the dark regions of the dead.

He guides our feet, He guards our way;
His morning smiles bless all the day;
He spreads the evening veil, and keeps
The silent hours while Israel sleeps.

Israel, a name divinely blest,
May rise secure, securely rest;
Thy holy Guardian's wakeful eyes
Admit no slumber nor surprise.

XCIX.

THERE is a land of pure delight,
  Where saints immortal reign,
Infinite day excludes the night,
  And pleasures banish pain.

There everlasting spring abides,
  And never-withering flowers;
Death, like a narrow sea, divides
  This heavenly land from ours.

Sweet fields beyond the swelling flood
  Stand dressed in living green:
So to the Jews old Canaan stood,
  While Jordan rolled between.

But timorous mortals start and shrink
  To cross this narrow sea,
And linger shivering on the brink,
  And fear to launch away.

O! could we make our doubts remove,
  These gloomy doubts that rise,
And see the Canaan that we love
  With unbeclouded eyes;

Could we but climb where Moses stood,
  And view the landscape o'er;
Not Jordan's stream, nor death's cold flood,
  Should fright us from the shore.

C.

THOU hidden Love of God, whose height,
  Whose depth unfathomed, no man knows:
I see from far Thy beauteous light,
  Inly I sigh for Thy repose:
My heart is pained, nor can it be
At rest, till it finds rest in Thee.

'Tis mercy all, that Thou hast brought
  My mind to seek her peace in Thee;
Yet while I seek, but find Thee not,
  No peace my wandering soul shall see;
O when shall all my wanderings end,
And all my steps to Thee-ward tend!

Is there a thing beneath the sun
  That strives with Thee my heart to share?
Ah, tear it thence, and reign alone,
  The Lord of every motion there!
Then shall my heart from earth be free,
When it hath found repose in Thee.

O hide this self from me, that I
  No more, but Christ in me, may live;
My vile affections crucify,
  Nor let one darling lust survive!
In all things nothing may I see,
Nothing desire or seek, but Thee!

Each moment draw from earth away
  My heart, that lowly waits Thy call;
Speak to my inmost soul, and say,
  "I am thy Love, thy God, thy All!"
To feel Thy power, to hear Thy voice,
To taste Thy love, be all my choice.

CI.

O FOR an heart to praise my God,
  An heart from sin set free!
An heart that always feels Thy blood,
  So freely spilt for me!

An heart resigned, submissive, meek,
  My dear Redeemer's throne;
Where only Christ is heard to speak,
  Where Jesus reigns alone.

An humble, lowly, contrite heart,
  Believing, true, and clean:
Which neither life nor death can part
  From Him that dwells within:

An heart in every thought renewed,
  And full of love divine;
Perfect, and right, and pure, and good,
  A copy, Lord, of Thine.

Thy nature, gracious Lord, impart;
  Come quickly from above;
Write Thy new name upon my heart,
  Thy new, blest name of love.

CII.

SOLDIERS of Christ, arise,
And put your armour on,
Strong in the strength which God supplies
Through His eternal Son:

Strong in the Lord of hosts,
And in His mighty power;
Who in the strength of Jesus trusts
Is more than conqueror.

Stand then in His great might,
With all His strength endued;
But take, to arm you for the fight,
The panoply of God.

From strength to strength go on,
Wrestle, and fight, and pray;
Tread all the powers of darkness down,
And win the well-fought day.

That having all things done,
And all your conflicts past,
Ye may o'ercome, through Christ alone,
And stand entire at last.

CIII.

O GOD, of good the unfathomed sea,
Who would not give his heart to Thee?
  Who would not love Thee with his might,
O Jesu, Lover of mankind?
Who would not his whole soul and mind,
  With all his strength, to Thee unite?

High throned on heaven's eternal hill,
In number, weight, and measure still
  Thou sweetly orderest all that is:
And yet Thou deign'st to come to me,
And guide my steps, that I, with Thee
  Enthroned, may reign in endless bliss.

Fountain of good, all blessing flows
From Thee: no want Thy fulness knows;
  What but Thyself canst Thou desire?
Yet, self-sufficient as Thou art,
Thou dost desire my worthless heart:
  This, only this, dost Thou require.

O God, of good the unfathomed sea,
Who would not give his heart to Thee?
  Who would not love Thee with his might,
O Jesu, Lover of mankind?
Who would not his whole soul and mind,
  With all his strength, to Thee unite?

CIV.

YE servants of the Lord,
  Each in his office wait,
Observant of His heavenly word,
  And watchful at His gate.

Let all your lamps be bright,
  And trim the golden flame;
Gird up your loins, as in His sight,
  For awful is His name.

Watch; 'tis your Lord's command;
  And, while we speak, He's near;
Mark the first signal of His hand,
  And ready all appear.

O happy servant he,
  In such a posture found!
He shall his Lord with rapture see,
  And be with honour crowned.

Christ shall the banquet spread
  With His own royal hand;
And raise that favourite servant's head
  Amid the angelic band.

CV.

SHINE on our souls, eternal God,
  With rays of beauty shine!
O let Thy favour crown our days,
  And all their round be Thine!

Did we not raise our hands to Thee,
  Our hands might toil in vain;
Small joy success itself could give,
  If Thou Thy love restrain.

With Thee let every week begin,
  With Thee each day be spent;
For Thee each fleeting hour improved,
  Since each by Thee is lent.

Thus cheer us through this desert road,
  Till all our labours cease,
And heaven refresh our weary souls
  With everlasting peace.

CVI.

O GOD of Bethel, by whose hand
  Thy people still are fed,
Who through this weary pilgrimage
  Hast all our fathers led;

Our vows, our prayers, we now present
  Before Thy throne of grace;
God of our fathers, be the God
  Of their succeeding race.

Through each perplexing path of life
  Our wandering footsteps guide;
Give us each day our daily bread,
  And raiment fit provide.

O spread Thy covering wings around
  Till all our wanderings cease,
And at our Father's loved abode
  Our souls arrive in peace!

Such blessings from Thy gracious hand
  Our humble prayers implore;
And Thou shalt be our chosen God,
  And portion evermore.

CVII.

WHILE with ceaseless course the sun
  Hasted through the former year,
Many souls their race have run,
  Never more to meet us here:
Fixed in an eternal state,
  They have done with all below;
We a little longer wait,
  But how little, none can know.

As the wingèd arrow flies
  Speedily the mark to find;
As the lightning from the skies
  Darts, and leaves no trace behind;
Swiftly thus our fleeting days
  Bear us down life's rapid stream:
Upward, Lord! our spirits raise;
  All below is but a dream.

Thanks for mercies past receive;
  Pardon of our sins renew;
Teach us, henceforth, how to live
  With eternity in view:
Bless Thy word to young and old;
  Fill us with a Saviour's love;
And when life's short tale is told,
  May we dwell with Thee above!

CVIII.

GLORIOUS things of thee are spoken,
  Zion, city of our God;
He, whose word cannot be broken,
  Formed thee for His own abode:
On the Rock of ages founded,
  What can shake thy sure repose?
With salvation's walls surrounded,
  Thou mayst smile at all thy foes.

See, the streams of living waters,
  Springing from eternal Love,
Well supply thy sons and daughters,
  And all fear of want remove:
Who can faint, while such a river
  Ever flows their thirst to assuage?
Grace, which, like the Lord the giver,
  Never fails from age to age.

CIX.

GOD moves in a mysterious way
  His wonders to perform;
He plants His footsteps in the sea,
  And rides upon the storm.

Deep in unfathomable mines
  Of never-failing skill,
He treasures up His bright designs,
  And works His sovereign will.

Ye fearful saints, fresh courage take;
  The clouds ye so much dread
Are big with mercy, and shall break
  In blessings on your head.

Judge not the Lord by feeble sense,
  But trust Him for His grace;
Behind a frowning Providence
  He hides a smiling face.

His purposes will ripen fast,
  Unfolding every hour;
The bud may have a bitter taste,
  But sweet will be the flower.

Blind unbelief is sure to err,
  And scan His work in vain;
God is His own interpreter,
  And He will make it plain.

CX.

JESUS, where'er Thy people meet,
There they behold Thy mercy-seat;
Where'er they seek Thee, Thou art found,
And every place is hallowed ground.

For Thou, within no walls confined,
Inhabitest the humble mind;
Such ever bring Thee where they come,
And going take Thee to their home.

Dear Shepherd of Thy chosen few,
Thy former mercies here renew;
Here to our waiting hearts proclaim
The sweetness of Thy saving name.

Here may we prove the power of prayer
To strengthen faith, and sweeten care,
To teach our faint desires to rise,
And bring all heaven before our eyes.

Lord, we are few, but Thou art near;
Nor short Thine arm, nor deaf Thine ear;
O rend the heavens, come quickly down,
And make a thousand hearts Thine own!

CXI.

WHERE high the heavenly temple stands,
The house of God not made with hands,
A great High Priest our nature wears,
The Patron of mankind appears.

He who for men in mercy stood,
And poured on earth His precious blood,
Pursues in heaven His plan of grace,
The guardian God of human race.

Though now ascended up on high,
He bends on earth a Brother's eye;
Partaker of the human name,
He knows the frailty of our frame.

Our Fellow-sufferer yet retains
A fellow-feeling of our pains;
And still remembers in the skies
His tears, His agonies, and cries.

In every pang that rends the heart
The Man of Sorrows had a part;
He sympathises with our grief,
And to the sufferer sends relief.

With boldness therefore, at the throne,
Let us make all our sorrows known;
And ask the aids of heavenly power
To help us in the evil hour.

CXII.

GUIDE us, Thou whose name is Saviour,
Pilgrims in the barren land;
We are weak, and Thou Almighty;
Hold us with Thy strong right hand,
As in Egypt,
As upon the Red Sea strand.

Let the cloud and fire supernal
Day and night before us go;
Lead us to the rock and fountain
Whence the living waters flow:
Bread of heaven,
Feed us, till no want we know.

When we touch the cold, dark river,
Cleave for us the swelling tide;
Through the flood and through the whirlpool
Let Thine ark our footsteps guide:
Jesu, lead us,
Land us safe on Canaan's side.

Praise the Father, God of heaven,
Him who reigns supreme on high;
Praise the Son, for sinners given,
E'en to suffer and to die;
Praise the Spirit,
Guiding us so lovingly.

CXIII.

HOSANNA to the living Lord!
Hosanna to the Incarnate Word!
To Christ, Creator, Saviour, King,
Let earth, let heaven, Hosanna sing.
  Hosanna, Lord, Hosanna in the highest!

"Hosanna, Lord," Thine angels cry;
"Hosanna, Lord," Thy saints reply:
Above, beneath us, and around,
The dead and living swell the sound.
  Hosanna, Lord, Hosanna in the highest!

O Saviour, with protecting care
Return to this Thy house of prayer,
Assembled in Thy sacred name,
Where we Thy parting promise claim.
  Hosanna, Lord, Hosanna in the highest!

But, chiefest, in our cleansèd breast,
Eternal! bid Thy Spirit rest;
And make our secret soul to be
A temple pure, and worthy Thee.
  Hosanna, Lord, Hosanna in the highest!

So, in the last and dreadful day,
When earth and heaven shall melt away,
Thy flock, redeemed from sinful stain,
Shall swell the sound of praise again,
  Hosanna, Lord, Hosanna in the highest!

CXIV.

MUCH in sorrow, oft in woe,
Onward, Christians, onward go;
Fight the fight, and, worn with strife,
Steep with tears the bread of life.

Onward, Christians, onward go;
Join the war, and face the foe;
Faint not! much doth yet remain;
Dreary is the long campaign.

Shrink not, Christians! will ye yield?
Will ye quit the painful field?
Will ye flee in danger's hour?
Know ye not your Captain's power?

Let your drooping hearts be glad;
March, in heavenly armour clad;
Fight, nor think the battle long;
Victory soon shall tune your song.

Let not sorrow dim your eye,
Soon shall every tear be dry;
Let not woe your course impede;
Great your strength, if great your need.

Onward then to battle move;
More than conquerors ye shall prove;
Though opposed by many a foe,
Christian soldiers, onward go!

CXV.

FROM Greenland's icy mountains,
  From India's coral strand,
Where Afric's sunny fountains
  Roll down their golden sand,
From many an ancient river,
  From many a palmy plain,
They call us to deliver
  Their land from error's chain.

What though the spicy breezes
  Blow soft o'er Java's isle;
Though every prospect pleases,
  And only man is vile?
In vain with lavish kindness
  The gifts of God are strown;
The heathen in his blindness
  Bows down to wood and stone.

Can we, whose souls are lighted
  With wisdom from on high,
Can we to men benighted
  The lamp of life deny?
Salvation! O salvation!
  The joyful sound proclaim,
Till each remotest nation
  Has learnt Messiah's name.

Waft, waft, ye winds, His story,
  And you, ye waters, roll,
Till like a sea of glory
  It spreads from pole to pole;
Till o'er our ransomed nature
  The Lamb for sinners slain,
Redeemer, King, Creator,
  In bliss returns to reign.

CXVI.

PRAISE the Lord! ye heavens, adore Him,
  Praise Him, angels, in the height;
Sun and moon, rejoice before Him,
  Praise Him, all ye stars and light:
Praise the Lord, for He hath spoken,
  Worlds His mighty voice obeyed;
Laws, which never shall be broken,
  For their guidance He hath made.

Praise the Lord! for He is glorious;
  Never shall His promise fail;
God hath made His saints victorious,
  Sin and death shall not prevail.
Praise the God of our salvation;
  Hosts on high, His power proclaim;
Heaven and earth, and all creation,
  Laud and magnify His name!

CXVII.

BLEST are the pure in heart,
For they shall see our God;
The secret of the Lord is theirs;
Their soul is Christ's abode.

The Lord, who left the heavens,
Our life and peace to bring,
To dwell in lowliness with men,
Their pattern and their King;

Still to the lowly soul
He doth Himself impart,
And for His dwelling and His throne
Chooseth the pure in heart.

Lord, we Thy presence seek;
May ours this blessing be;
Give us a pure and lowly heart,
A temple meet for Thee.

CXVIII.

WHEN our heads are bowed with woe,
When our bitter tears o'erflow,
When we mourn the lost, the dear,
Gracious Son of Mary, hear!

Thou our throbbing flesh hast worn,
Thou our mortal griefs hast borne,
Thou hast shed the human tear;
Gracious Son of Mary, hear!

When the sullen death-bell tolls
For our own departed souls,
When our final doom is near,
Gracious Son of Mary, hear!

Thou hast bowed the dying head,
Thou the blood of life hast shed,
Thou hast filled a mortal bier;
Gracious Son of Mary, hear!

When the heart is sad within
With the thought of all its sin,
When the spirit shrinks with fear,
Gracious Son of Mary, hear!

Thou the shame, the grief hast known,
Though the sins were not Thine own,
Thou hast deigned their load to bear;
Gracious Son of Mary, hear!

CXIX.

LEAD, kindly Light, amid the encircling gloom,
Lead Thou me on!
The night is dark, and I am far from home;
Lead Thou me on!
Keep Thou my feet; I do not ask to see
The distant scene; one step enough for me.

I was not ever thus, nor prayed that Thou
Shouldst lead me on;
I loved to choose and see my path; but now
Lead Thou me on!
I loved the garish day, and, spite of fears,
Pride ruled my will: remember not past years.

So long Thy power has blest me, sure it still
Will lead me on
O'er moor and fen, o'er crag and torrent, till
The night is gone,
And with the morn those angel faces smile
Which I have loved long since, and lost awhile!

CXX.

WE saw Thee not when Thou didst come
  To this poor world of sin and death,
Nor e'er beheld Thy cottage-home
  In that despisèd Nazareth;
But we believe Thy footsteps trod
Its streets and plains, Thou Son of God.

We did not see Thee lifted high
  Amid that wild and savage crew,
Nor heard Thy meek, imploring cry,
  "Forgive, they know not what they do;"
Yet we believe the deed was done,
Which shook the earth, and veiled the sun.

We stood not by the empty tomb
  Where late Thy sacred Body lay;
Nor sat within that upper room,
  Nor met Thee in the open way:
But we believe that angels said,
"Why seek the living 'midst the dead?"

We did not mark the chosen few,
  When Thou didst through the clouds ascend,
First lift to heaven their wondering view,
  Then to the earth all prostrate bend;
Yet we believe that mortal eyes
Beheld Thee mount beyond the skies.

And now that Thou dost reign above,
  And thence Thy faithful people bless,
No outward glory from Thy love
  Doth shine upon our wilderness:
But we believe Thy faithful word,
And wait for our returning Lord.

CXXI.

HARK, hark, my soul! angelic songs are swelling
O'er earth's green fields, and ocean's wave-beat shore:
How sweet the truth those blessed strains are telling
Of that new life when sin shall be no more!
Angels of Jesus, angels of light,
Singing to welcome the pilgrims of the night.

Onward we go, for still we hear them singing,
"Come, weary souls, for Jesus bids you come:"
And, through the dark its echoes sweetly ringing,
The music of the Gospel leads us home.
Angels of Jesus, angels of light,
Singing to welcome the pilgrims of the night.

Far, far away, like bells at evening pealing,
The voice of Jesus sounds o'er land and sea,
And laden souls by thousands meekly stealing,
Kind Shepherd, turn their weary steps to Thee.
Angels of Jesus, angels of light,
Singing to welcome the pilgrims of the night.

Rest comes at length, though life be long and dreary,
The day must dawn, and darksome night be past;
All journeys end in welcome to the weary,
And heaven, the heart's true home, will come at last.
Angels of Jesus, angels of light,
Singing to welcome the pilgrims of the night.

Angels, sing on! your faithful watches keeping;
  Sing us sweet fragments of the songs above;
Till morning's joy shall end the night of weeping,
  And life's long shadows break in endless love.
Angels of Jesus, angels of light,
Singing to welcome the pilgrims of the night.

CXXII.

THY way, not mine, O Lord,
  However dark it be!
Lead me by Thine own hand,
  Choose out the path for me.

Smooth let it be or rough,
  It will be still the best;
Winding or straight, it leads
  Right onward to Thy rest.

I dare not choose my lot;
  I would not, if I might;
Choose Thou for me, my God,
  So shall I walk aright.

The kingdom that I seek
  Is Thine; so let the way
That leads to it be Thine,
  Else I must surely stray.

Take Thou my cup, and it
  With joy or sorrow fill,
As best to Thee may seem;
  Choose Thou my good and ill.

Choose Thou for me my friends,
  My sickness or my health;
Choose Thou my cares for me,
  My poverty or wealth.

Not mine, not mine the choice,
  In things or great or small;
Be Thou my guide, my strength,
  My wisdom, and my all.

CXXIII.

MY God and Father, while I stray,
Far from my home, on life's rough way,
O teach me from my heart to say
"Thy will be done."

Though dark my path, and sad my lot,
Let me be still and murmur not,
Or breathe the prayer divinely taught,
"Thy will be done."

What though in lonely grief I sigh
For friends beloved, no longer nigh,
Submissive would I still reply,
"Thy will be done."

If Thou shouldst call me to resign
What most I prize, it ne'er was mine;
I only yield Thee what is Thine;
"Thy will be done."

Let but my fainting heart be blest
With Thy sweet Spirit for its guest,
My God, to Thee I leave the rest;
"Thy will be done."

Renew my will from day to day,
Blend it with Thine, and take away
All that now makes it hard to say
"Thy will be done."

CXXIV.

THE Church's one foundation
  Is Jesus Christ her Lord;
She is His new creation
  By water and the Word:
From heaven He came and sought her
  To be His holy Bride,
With His own blood He bought her,
  And for her life He died.

Elect from every nation,
  Yet one o'er all the earth,
Her charter of salvation
  One Lord, one faith, one birth;
One holy Name she blesses,
  Partakes one holy Food,
And to one hope she presses
  With every grace endued.

Mid toil, and tribulation,
  And tumult of her war,
She waits the consummation
  Of peace for evermore;
Till with the vision glorious
  Her longing eyes are blest,
And the great Church victorious
  Shall be the Church at rest.

INDEX OF AUTHORS,[*] &c.

The Delegates of the Clarendon Press, to whom has been entrusted the task of preparing this Hymnal, acknowledge the permission kindly granted by various living authors, and by representatives of authors, for the insertion of hymns of which they possess the copyright.

OXFORD, *Easter*, 1872.

I.—Sir W. Scott, 'Lay of the Last Minstrel;' based on the *Dies iræ*.

II.—The first ten verses of the *Prosa de Mortuis*, or *De die Judicii*, probably by Thomas of Celano, a Franciscan of the thirteenth century. Original of line 3, *Teste David cum Sibylla:* in the later French church was substituted, *Crucis expandens vexilla*.

III.—John Cennick, Rev. Charles Wesley, Martin Madan, composed various parts of this hymn.

IV.—Philip Doddridge, D.D., 1755.

V.—Part by W. B. Collyer, 1812. Original of stanza 2, line 3,

And greet the Archangel's warning,
To meet their Saviour in the skies
On this auspicious morning.

VI.—Rev. Joseph Anstice, 1836.

VII.—*Jordanis oras*, an Advent hymn in the Parisian Breviary; translated by the Rev. J. Chandler.

VIII.—Horatius Bonar, D.D., 'Lays of Faith and Hope.' Inserted by permission of Messrs. Nisbet and Co.

IX.—John Milton; part of his hymn on the Nativity.

X.—Of the fifteenth or sixteenth century: said to be of Cistercian origin.

XI.—Aurelius Prudentius Clemens (about A.D. 400): from the *Hymnus omnis horæ*, in his 'Cathemerinōn,' except the doxology, which is later. Original of stanza 3, lines 3, 4,

> Dexter in Parentis arce
> Qui cluis virtutibus.

XII.—Rev. Charles Wesley, 1743, and Martin Madan, 1760. Original of stanza 1, lines 1, 2,

> Hark, how all the welkin rings,
> Glory to the King of kings!

Original of stanza 2, lines 7, 8,

> Pleased as Man with men to appear,
> Jesus our Immanuel here.

XIII.—Nahum Tate, D.D., 1703.

XIV.—St. Ambrose (ob. A.D. 397): Doxology later.

XV.—Ascribed to St. Bernard (ob. A.D. 1153). See Daniel, Thes. Hymnol. i. 227, iv. 215.

XVI.—From a hymn by Rev. John Newton, 1779.

XVII.—Jonas Scheffler ('Angelus Silesius'), 1657: translated by Catharine Winkworth.

XVIII.—From a hymn by James Montgomery, 1822.

XIX.—W. Chatterton Dix, 1860.

XX.—T. Sternhold: part of Old Version of Ps. xxv. Original of stanza 1, lines 2, 3, 4,

> I pray Thee, Lord, remember,
> And eke Thy pity plentiful,
> For they have been for ever.

XXI.—A re-casting of John Mardley's 'Lamentation of a Sinner,' mostly by Nahum Tate, D.D.: part by Bishop Heber.

XXII.—Part of New Version of Ps. li.

XXIII.—New Version of Ps. cxxx.

XXIV.—Isaac Watts, D.D., 1709.

XXV.—Rev. Charles Wesley, 1740.

XXVI.—Part of a hymn by Rev. Aug. M. Toplady, 1776.

XXVII.—John Morrison, 1770.

XXVIII.—Sir Robert Grant, 1815.

XXIX.—Bishop Heber, 1827.

XXX.—Dean Milman, 1827. Inserted by permission of Mr. Murray.

XXXI.—Dean Milman. Inserted by permission of Mr. Murray.

XXXII.—Rev. Isaac Williams: from his 'Baptistery.' Original of stanza 2, lines 1, 2, 'me' for 'us;' stanza 3, lines 1, 2,

> Supplication on us pour,
> Let us now knock at the door.

Original of stanza 6, line 1,

> 'Neath thy wings let us have place.

XXXIII.—J. H. Newman, D.D.: from his 'Verses on various Occasions.'

XXXIV.—*Ad regias Agni dapes*, in Roman Breviary for 'Dominica in Albis:' an altered form of the very ancient *Ad cœnam Agni providi*, which was a hymn for the Easter Communion of the new-baptized. Translation combined from R. Campbell and 'Hymns Ancient and Modern.' (By permission of the Editors.)

XXXV.—Author unknown: eighteenth century.

XXXVI.—Author unknown. In Daniel, Thes. Hymn. ii. 363.

XXXVII.—C. F. Gellert, a German hymn-writer of the eighteenth century: translated by Frances E. Cox.

XXXVIII.—Rev. C. Wesley.

XXXIX.—Part of a poem *De contemptu mundi*, by Bernard de Morlaix, a Cluniac monk in the twelfth century. Translated by Dr. Neale: he wrote in stanza 4, line 1, 'The Cross;' in stanza 5, line 2, 'conjubilant;' in stanza 6, lines 1, 2,

> And who beneath their Leader
> Have conquered in the fight.

XL.—*Nobis Olympo redditus*, an Ascension hymn in the Parisian Breviary: translated by Rev. J. Chandler.

XLI.—Part of a hymn by Rev. C. Wesley. Original of stanza 6, line 1,

Grant, though parted from our sight.

XLII.—Emma Toke, 1851.

XLIII.—Dean Stanley.

XLIV.—Author unknown, but probably of the time of Charles the Great. See Daniel, Thes. Hymn. iv. 125.

XLV.—Variously ascribed to Robert II. King of France, Pope Innocent III. and Archbishop Stephen Langton; commonly called 'the Golden Sequence.' In Roman Missal.

XLVI.—Translation of No. 44, in 'Ordering of Priests.' Probably by Bishop Cosin; it appeared first in his 'Private Devotions,' and was inserted in the Ordinal in 1661.

XLVII.—Rev. R. W. Kyle, 1842.

XLVIII.—Rev. John Keble, 1827: 'Christian Year.'

XLIX.—Harriet Auber, 1829.

L.—Rev. F. Oakeley: part of a Trinity hymn in his 'Lyra Liturgica.'

LI.—Bishop Heber.

LII.—Rev. A. T. Russell, 1848.

LIII.—Theod. Schenk, a German hymn writer, 1727: translated by Frances E. Cox.

LIV.—W. E. Cameron, 1770: one of the 'Scotch Paraphrases.'

LV.—Bishop Heber.

LVI.—Part of a hymn by Rev. C. Wesley.

LVII.—St. Thomas Aquinas, ob. 1274: part of his 'Eucharistic Sequence.' In Roman Missal, for Corpus Christi.

LVIII.—P. Doddridge, D.D.

LIX.—Josiah Conder, 1824.

LX.—Edw. Osler, 1836.

LXI.—Prudentius: four stanzas from 'Cathemerinōn,' i. ('Hymn at Cock-crowing'): Doxology later. Roman Breviary, Tuesday.

LXII.—Prudentius: from 'Cathemerinōn,' ii. ('Morning Hymn'): third stanza as made up in Roman Breviary for Wednesday, from several stanzas.

LXIII.—The 29th of the hymns called 'Ambrosian.' Roman Breviary, Prime.

LXIV.—Bishop Ken, ob. 1712. From his Morning Hymn.

LXV.—Bishop Ken: from the same.

LXVI.—Rev. C. Wesley.

LXVII.—Isaac Watts, D.D.

LXVIII.—Rev. J. Keble: 'Christian Year.'

LXIX.—*Nunc Sancte nobis*, the 21st 'Ambrosian' hymn; Roman Breviary, Terce; translated by Dr. Newman.

LXX.—*Rector potens*, the 22nd Ambrosian hymn; Roman Breviary, None: translated by Dr. Newman.

LXXI.—*Prono volutus*, the hymn for None in the Parisian Breviary: translated by Rev. J. Chandler.

LXXII.—*Φῶς ἱλαρὸν ἁγίας δόξης*, the Vesper Hymn of the Eastern Church. Probably of the second or third century; referred to as 'ancient' by St. Basil, De Spir. Sanct. s. 73. See it in Routh, Rell. Sacr. iii. 515. Translated by W. Bright, D.D.

LXXIII.—Bishop Ken.

LXXIV.—First stanza by Bishop Heber; second by Archbishop Whately.

LXXV.—Rev. J. Keble: 'Christian Year.'

LXXVI.—Rev. H. F. Lyte, 1847. (Written during consumption.) Extracted, by permission of Messrs. Rivington, from the author's 'Miscellaneous Poems.'

LXXVII.—Stephen 'the Sabaite,' an Eastern monk of the eighth century: translated by J. M. Neale, D.D.

LXXVIII.—Frederick W. Faber, D.D.

LXXIX.—Part of Bernard de Morlaix's poem. (See above, Hymn 39.) Translated by Dr. Neale.

LXXX.—T. Sternhold: part of Old Version of Ps. xviii.

LXXXI.—John Hopkins. Old Version of Ps. c.

LXXXII.—From Paul Gerhardt (seventeenth century): translated by Rev. J. Wesley.

LXXXIII.—New Version of Ps. viii.

LXXXIV.—Part of New Version of Ps. lxvii.

LXXXV.—Part of New Version of Ps. lxxxiv.

LXXXVI.—Dr. Watts: paraphrase of Ps. xciii.

LXXXVII.—Part of New Version of Ps. xcv.

LXXXVIII.—Part of New Version of Ps. ciii.

LXXXIX.—Part of New Version of Ps. cxxxix.

XC.—Part of New Version of Ps. cxlix.

XCI.—Joseph Addison: paraphrase of Ps. xix.

XCII.—Joseph Addison : part of his paraphrase of Ps. xxiii.

XCIII.—Joseph Addison.

XCIV.—A Latin version of Ps. cxvii.; writer unknown.

XCV.—A paraphrase of Ps. cxxx., in New College Anthem-book.

XCVI.—Dr. Watts, and Rev. C. Wesley: paraphrase of Ps. c.

XCVII.—Dr. Watts: part of paraphrase of Ps. xc.

XCVIII.—Dr. Watts: part of paraphrase of Ps. cxxi.

XCIX.—Dr. Watts.

C.—Rev. C. Wesley.

CI.—Rev. C. Wesley.

CII.—Rev. C. Wesley: part of a long poem.

CIII.—Rev. C. Wesley.

CIV.—P. Doddridge, D.D.

CV.—Dr. Doddridge.

CVI.—Dr. Doddridge, and J. Logan.

CVII.—Rev. John Newton.

CVIII.—Rev. J. Newton: paraphrase of Ps. lxxxvii.

CIX.—W. Cowper.

CX.—W. Cowper.

CXI.—Michael Bruce: paraphrase of Heb. iv. 14 sq.

CXII.—Rev. J. Keble. A re-casting of the hymn 'Guide me, O Thou great Jehovah,' by W. Williams, 1774.

CXIII.—Bishop Heber.

CXIV.—H. K. White, 1806, and Fanny F. Maitland, 1827.

CXV.—Bishop Heber.

CXVI.—Bishop Mant: based on Ps. cxlviii.

CXVII.—Stanzas 1 and 3 by Rev. J. Keble: 'Christian Year.'

CXVIII.—Dean Milman. Inserted by permission of Mr. Murray.

CXIX.—J. H. Newman, D.D.

CXX.—Rev. J. H. Gurney.

CXXI.—Frederick Faber, D.D. Original of stanza 5, lines 3, 4,

While we toil on, and soothe ourselves with weeping,
Till life's long night shall break in endless love.

CXXII.—Horatius Bonar, D.D. Inserted by permission of Messrs. Nisbet & Co.

CXXIII.—Charlotte Elliott. Original of stanza 4, lines 1, 2, 3,

Though Thou hast called me to resign
What most I prized, it ne'er was mine;
I have but yielded what was Thine.

CXXIV.—Rev. S. J. Stone.

*** Much information as to sources of Hymns will be found in Sir R. Palmer's 'Book of Praise,' and the Rev. L. C. Biggs's edition of 'Hymns Ancient and Modern.'

INDEX OF FIRST LINES.